# ESCAPE

## A QUEER NOVEL AT SEA

# ESCAPE

## A QUEER NOVEL AT SEA

## MILES CIGOLLE

SUNSTONE PRESS
SANTA FE

Sunstone books may be purchased for educational, business, or sales promotional use. For information please write: Special Markets Department, Sunstone Press, P.O. Box 2321, Santa Fe, New Mexico 87504-2321.
Printed on acid-free paper
∞
eBook: 978-1-61139-763-5

Library of Congress Cataloging-in-Publication Data

Names: Cigolle, Miles, author.
Title: Escape : a queer novel at sea / Miles Cigolle.
Description: Santa Fe : Sunstone Press, 2025. | Summary: "In this queer novel on a ten-day deluxe gay cruise on the Jolly Roger, Miles discovers life and death, love and betrayal and finally truth and redemption"-- Provided by publisher.
Identifiers: LCCN 2024058004 | ISBN 9781632937438 (paperback ; acid-free paper) | ISBN 9781611397635 (epub)
Subjects: LCGFT: Queer fiction. | Novels.
Classification: LCC PS3603.I354 E83 2025 | DDC 813/.6--dc23/eng/20241203
LC record available at https://lccn.loc.gov/2024058004

**WWW.SUNSTONEPRESS.COM**
SUNSTONE PRESS / POST OFFICE BOX 2321 / SANTA FE, NM 87504-2321 /USA
(505) 988-4418

# PREFACE

The ultimate Escape. It's unlike any experience you'll ever have. Ten days onboard the pristine Art Deco ocean liner, the Jolly Roger, in the middle of the picture-postcard Adriatic Sea. That and two hundred of the hottest gay men on the planet, gym bods on the prowl. Captain Brook is in charge, although his trans wife Mrs. J really calls the shots. Miles will be your knowledgeable on-land guide, his sweetheart Abbey is onboard along with several very tall drag queens, the love birds Toby and Troy, a half dozen butch exhibitionists, one wayward Catholic priest and Miles's cousin the sweet nun Sister Sofia. Of course more than a few S&M wannabees, plus two sex club go-go boys Ebony and Mohawk. I forgot to mention moody Dylan, but he doesn't really count. Don't believe everything you read. The best thing about an escape is leaving your past behind. It's a chance to cleanse the soul and be reborn.

Welcome aboard all you Lost Boys.

# DAY 1:
# MONDAY — ARRIVAL VENICE

All gay men have at least considered it. But it is so expensive few guys can afford it. So it remains an elusive dream.

The only reason Abbey and I signed on for this ten-day Brand Q cruise was because of Toby. He wanted to see Croatia, Dubrovnik and the stash of Caravaggio paintings in Malta. It's on Toby's bucket list of essential things to do before he dies. You see Toby is on disability with full blown AIDS and has calculated the exact number of days he has left to play world traveler. Last year he and Dylan did a ten-day cruise of the Nile. Toby even rode on a camel and saw the inside of a pyramid. Since last year, Toby's health has declined further. He's slowly going blind. So this year Toby chose a cruise that starts in Venice and ends in Malta. It will be his first all-gay cruise. Toby confided in me that the all-gay thing makes him a little nervous; but he knows he'll probably be blind in another year, so he wants to see as many hot men and as much hard dick while he still has his vision. I don't blame the poor guy.

This time Toby chose a high-end deluxe Brand Q cruise. Two hundred queens maximum onboard a gorgeous Art Deco ocean liner, The Jolly Roger. How apropos given all those Lost Boys onboard. It's more like a very large yacht, just three smallish decks, a huge central pool and a pair of small orgy hot tubs. It will mark Abbey and my first gay cruise. Besides my Cornell buddy Toby and his lover Dylan, our pals from the Pines, the retired school teachers Mac and Ray and the lawyers Murry and Richard will be joining us.

Toby booked the night before our cruise departure in Venice at the Danieli. Actually Toby wanted to book two nights but Dylan protested. Dylan is cheap. He's a banker working for a Swiss bank.

He makes plenty, twice Toby's disability check. But Dylan is as tight as a duck's ass. So Abbey and I are on our own tonight. Toby and Dylan will show up in the morning.

The Danieli was unbelievable. At two-thousand-dollars a night it better be. It's practically next door to the Doge's Palace facing the Lagoon. The salmon-colored Gothic façade reeks of Venice. It's large terraces framed in white stone face the morning sunlight. It's magical. We asked for a room on the top floor with views to Palladio's famous churches. The center lobby was dominated by an imposing marble staircase flooded with natural light. The walls of the three-story lobby were giant slabs of book-matched colored marble. It's an architectural feast, a smorgasbord of questionable taste. The main flower bouquet at the base of the grand stair must have been at least five-feet in diameter with an acre's worth of freshly cut flowers. Attendants in crisp uniforms were waiting in every corner. The arrival of two party-boy faggots dressed in leather didn't go unnoticed. The tall bell boy assigned to us smiled warmly. In the elevator up to the top floor he introduced himself as Giuseppe. His broken English was adorable. "Welcome to Venice. Bene, are you here Brand Q gay cruise? Si, mia brother works on boat. Si bene." With that declaration Giuseppe gave his hot crotch a good hard squeeze. I was already semi-erect. Inside the room, I locked the door and the three of us went oral. Giuseppe had a gorgeous Venetian cock. We gave him a double header blowjob and a double tip. He parted with a smile offering to arrange our transport to our boat the morning of our departure. The Danieli was as queer as a three-dollar bill, perfect for this pampered crowd.

After a light lunch in the hotel Palm Court, Abbey and I headed off to the Ospedale Dela Pieta, the Venetian convent, orphanage and music school established by Antonio Vivaldi himself ages ago to serve orphans and abandoned girls. I was eager to meet my cousin Sister Sofia. I was hoping to find out if the orphanage had any beds for AIDS patients. I had read in the NY Times that some Catholic hospitals in Italy were quietly placing PWAs inside their facilities. I was hopeful my cousin could tell me. As soon as I saw Sister Sofia's face I knew we were in good hands. There was a small pilot program which she oversees. In an abandoned wing on an upper floor she secretly cares for a dozen PWAs, just trying to comfort them a little as they die slowly. There are no treatments. I started crying. Sister Sofia introduced us to each of the men. I gave each one a gentle hug, a kiss on their heads. They smiled back so happy to meet both of us, queers from America. When we told them about our upcoming gay men's cruise they laughed with tears. It was sad and beautiful. Parting with my cousin was the most emotional. "Are you taking good care of yourself Miles? Do you practice safer sex? You know I love you and Abbey. You are always in my daily prayers. Please be careful." I had never told her I was HIV+. It was not necessary. I was one of the lucky ones. I had the best doctors and the best care. I was doing fine up to this point. Beyond that all bets were off. Abbey still worked at AmFAR, the American Foundation for AIDS Research. He was on the front lines every day making sure I was okay. I was a very lucky man; I was a survivor.

# DAY 2:
## TUESDAY — DEPARTURE

Toby and Dylan arrived right on schedule. After an early breakfast the next morning Toby, Abbey and I were off to the Fortuny Museum. It's housed in the imposing 15th century Venetian Palazzo Pesaro, former home to the commander-in-chief of the Venetian navy. The colorful artist Mariano Fortuny called it home and the museum in his name today contains a fascinating collection reflecting Fortuny's varied interests in painting, set design, lighting design, fabrics and ladies' luxurious gowns. If he wasn't a faggot, I'm not gay. Toby is a major fan. Fortuny's over-the-top designs appealed to Toby's taste which leans towards the extravagant and slightly vulgar. The museum on two floors reflects Fortuny's artsy world which included a close friendship with Richard Wagner. Fortuny designed the stage sets for Wagner's Tristan and Isolde which premiered at La Scala in Milan. The museum retains a hoity-toity attitude today which appealed particularly to Toby's sense of exclusivity. Toby started heavy flirting with the clearly well-hung guard on the second floor. They ended up in a private toilet, with Toby's dick up the guy's hot Venetian ass. The used condom in the waste basket may have caused a bit of a scandal later on that morning.

After that unexpected sex adventure Toby and I met up with Abbey and Dylan back at the Danieli breakfast room. Dylan looked sour; his straw hat had been misplaced. But dear Giuseppe saved the day as he walked into the dining room handing the hat to Dylan. In usual fashion, Dylan hardly thanked him. Giuseppe also handed me a card with the name and number of his older brother Pedro on it. Giuseppe suggested we give Pedro a call once we get settled onboard the Jolly Roger. Turns out Pedro is also gay. It seems all of Venice is queer. Pedro works in the main engine room. Abbey's ears perked up at that news. He had already announced earlier that a tour of the engine room was at the top of his bucket list. He was ecstatic. Abbey kept the card in his front pocket. If Pedro looks anything like Giuseppe, we're in for a treat. Abbey and I gave Giuseppe a parting group hug. The private Danieli water taxi took us to the remote dock set up for ocean liners. Since Abbey and I were in Venice over twenty-five years ago, Venetian cruise ships have more than doubled in size. The Jolly Roger looked like a toy boat when parked next to these behemoths.

The scene at the Brand Q check-in said it all. This was going to be a gay experience. Not Carnival Cruises by any stretch of the imagination. Brand Q was going to be 100% queer. Well close, but not exactly.

Captain Brook who was standing at attention at the head of the line was as straight as they come; a real jock, he was a football quarterback at Cornell before he joined the Navy. I knew his wife Jackie from a Brand Q cruise Abbey and I took to Peru five years ago. Jackie or Mrs. J as she likes to be called, is the official Director of Social Activities at Brand Q. We have no problem with either of them. Brook has medals from the Navy plastered all over his crisp white Captain's uniform. He looks official. What the boys really tune into is his super-hot butt, pure USDA Prime. Plenty of gay guys have tried to get inside his white Captain's uniform. But Brook always plays it cool. He enjoys all the sexual attention. He just brushes the queers off like flies as he adjusts the position of his semi-erect cock inside his skin-tight chinos. Brook is as straight as an arrow. Actually Brook and Jackie make a very sexy straight couple. Mrs. J is a real hoot, a real fag hag, she loves to trade dirty jokes with the boys.

Actually there's a whole other side to Mrs. J. that few guys know about. Mrs. J was originally Jerry. We met him years ago on the Brand Q cruise to Peru. He was the head waiter in the main dining room. We bonded right away. He loved to flirt with all the guys. Abbey had the hots for his gorgeous ass like everyone else. So we proposed a steamy threesome. Afterwards, Jerry confided that he was about to pursue gender-affirming surgery to finally become a woman. It was already scheduled back in New York. It made total sense. We already knew from our threesome that he was strictly a bottom during sex. Plus he was the most flamboyant queen we'd ever met. His secret surgery was a huge success. As a confident new woman, she landed the new job as Brand Q's Director of Social Activities. A perfect fit, she knew how to handle fussy queens. After the surgery she enjoyed the best of both worlds in bed: gay men looking for a tight buttfuck and straight men looking for some hot pussy. Fortunately, that was about the time she met up with Brand Q's Captain Brook who fell for her overnight. He was the man of her dreams; end of story.

Anyway, we were really happy to see both of them again. We were in good hands. We traded warm hugs all around. Brook gave Abbey and me little welcome aboard pats on the ass. He's cool. Mrs. J practically raped Abbey and I. She had her hands all over us. She couldn't stop smiling.

Next we ran into our friends Mac and Ray from the Pines. They looked terrific. They had a cute bell boy in tow with at least half a dozen pieces of their Louis Vuitton luggage. They're filthy rich but super-nice. Mac is a leather queen and he's as anal as me. Ray invited us over for drinks later. They are in Premier First Class on the upper deck. Their spacious deck even has a private hot tub that easily accommodates four. "Wear your Speedos Miles. You know Mac likes to play footsie with your gorgeous cock." Mac and Ray always have sex on the brain. That's no problem with us.

Years ago when we first met Mac and Ray, we went together on a deluxe week-long tour of Chicago arranged through the National Historic Trust. Mac and Ray spent practically the whole trip in the hotel bed in their leather harnesses, slapping a leather paddle while watching porno and eating meals delivered to their door by room service. They fucked through the hour tour of Frank Lloyd Wright's Robie House. They told us they'd both already seen it twice before. I adore Ray. He's a father figure. He's older and wiser, really beautiful. He's a retired brilliant graphic designer; he was a major player on Madison Avenue in his prime. He likes the fact that I'm an architect with a celebrity architectural firm; which means I get to travel around the world. Ray is your sophisticated faggot.

I just saw Murray and Richard in the line behind us. Murray looks stressed out. I waved them up to join us in the line. Nobody cares. It's no problem cutting in. Everyone is relaxed and super friendly. They're already in cruise mode. Richard said they hit traffic leaving Rome with the kids. Seth and Sophie will be staying with Murray's mom in Verona while Murray and Richard are on the cruise. It's the first time they've traveled just by themselves since they adopted the kids nearly a decade ago. They're great kids and Murray and Richard are role model gay parents. It's beautiful to watch from the side lines.

Once they clear us to board they hand us a stem glass of champagne and offer a tray of canapes. Attendants silently whisk away our luggage to the safety of our rooms. How they know our names and cabin numbers remains a mystery. The open deck is soon crowded with guys sunning themselves in their Speedos or colored jockstraps, swaying to the club music, checking out the gym bods all around them. Abbey's moving instantly taking off his t-shirt. Toby and I join in. It's intoxicating. The men are super-hot. They exceed my expectations. Dylan takes a seat on the edge. He's frowning as if this is all too tacky for his sophisticated taste.

The sea of oiled male bodies parts briefly, revealing a stunning Black prince, clean shaven with a shiny bald head and gorgeous sapphire baby blues. His milk-chocolate colored skin is lightly oiled to pick up the highlights. He's definitely GQ model material. I immediately recall the Black stud in the men's showers as a boy back in my parent's pool club in Albuquerque. I obsessed over him my whole boyhood. Our Mr. Ebony was equally well hung. Through the white spandex I could easily make out his massive horizontal tool; it must be close to nine inches. As he turned I caught a glimpse of his beautiful rump. Hands down he was the most perfect specimen onboard. Absolutely. Right behind this guy must be his lucky lover. He's at close range guarding the family jewels. Taller, hairless and pale blond, he's wearing a large white Mohawk wig that makes him tower over the crowd. Together these two look like the perfect couple for a hot biracial sex scene with Ebony's tool down Mohawk's hungry throat.

We located our cabin on the middle deck. It had a tiny terrace and a cool round nautical window. I hid the usual extraneous hotel crap in the back of a drawer and adjusted the lighting. Our cabin was now perfect. We had raunchy butt sex in the tiny shower. It was extra hot. We were both horny from being around all these sexy studs in colored jockstraps. Our nap was interrupted by a phone call from Mac and Ray. We were invited for a light room-service dinner and a soak in their hot tub. "Absolutely." Dylan was too tired and bowed out. Count Toby, Abbey and I in. "Just be sure to wear your Speedos, or better yet come nude. You know we're casual here." When I opened the cracked door Mac and Ray were already in the hot tub donning their black leather harnesses. "Welcome boys! Grab a wrap. The water temp is perfect. Miles, get your pretty butt over here. You know how I like it." "Yes sir!" Mac always wants to fuck me. I never complain since he's a pro. Abbey and Toby gladly paired up. This time was hardly their first. Ray wanted to just play voyeur and take it all in visually. We all had a good time. Mac and Ray are simply the best. Egoless.

Abbey and I said good night to our buddies. Pausing on the main deck to take in the sunset, we heard Captain Brook's send-off orders loud and clear. "Let's take the boys to Sea!" The Jolly Roger was soon headed overnight to our first destination next morning, the small medieval town of Rovinj in Croatia. But before turning in I knew Abbey wanted to take a peek in the engine room. He still had Pedro's number safe in his front pocket. Pedro picked up right away. He was waiting for our call. We met Pedro outside the engine room door. He was just as cute as his younger brother Giuseppe, even cuter in his olive-colored work overalls. The tour lasted an hour. Abbey was terribly impressed. On the way out we offered Pedro a big cash tip. He shook his head back and forth and then squeezed his crotch while showing us his beautiful broad smile. "Bene bene Pompino. Bene bene Pompino." Being an out gay man, I happen to know pompino is Italian for blowjob. Abbey and I serviced Pedro properly, taking turns with his dick, taking our good time. It was an honor. What a beautiful Italian cock, thick just like his brother's. We parted with warm hugs. Using his hands gesturing, Pedro invited us back for another tour and more pompino anytime. We'll be back for both.

Suddenly, over the public address system we heard Mrs. J's distinctive high voice. "Ladies and Gentlemen welcome to the

Trans Welcome Dance. As the first openly trans employee at Brand Q. I'd like to welcome each of you beautiful souls to the main deck. Let's celebrate our uniqueness. Free refreshments and music to fall in love by. Let's greet each other and party! I love each of you, my trans brothers and sisters!" I was so impressed with Jackie. The whole thing was her idea. Over a hundred guys and gals showed up, a good half of the passengers onboard the Jolly Roger. Captain Brook made the rounds hugging everyone, telling jokes and stories. It was emotional for many of them. They had never been welcomed onboard before. For them this cruise was a big deal. It was about more than just sex. It was about self-discovery, about being true to oneself. For many it was the first hurdle of their new identity, their brave new journey in a world that was often hostile.

Back in our cabin we had another surprise. While we were out dancing on the main deck with Jackie and her friends, the chamber maid had turned down our beds for the night. Pure Brand Q. Instead of chocolates under the pillows, she carefully arranged four new condoms on top of each of our pillows. Sweet dreams.

# DAY 3:
# WEDNESDAY — ROVINJ, CROATIA

Over breakfast Toby told Abbey and I that Dylan showed up in their cabin at four o'clock in the morning completely inebriated, his head in the toilet bowl. After we left him on the dance floor of the main deck he apparently spent the remainder of the evening drinking booze nonstop in the bar Last Call on the lower deck. He's taken to carrying a pocket flask for vodka or gin. Toby said it's the only thing that keeps him even barely sociable. When he's sober, he's a nasty jaded old queen, especially toward women who he treats with contempt for no apparent reason. If a female stranger accidently offends him for some reason, look out, he attacks them verbally. He'll mock them; until he makes them cry. He's a classic misogynist.

Toby turned quiet. I could see he was very upset. When he finally spoke he was on the verge of tears. "Dylan is full of anger. He's furious at the world, especially at me because I have AIDS. Sometimes I feel like he wants to strangle me. He blames me a hundred percent. It's all my fault. It's bad enough I've infected myself through my out-of-control behavior. I've also dragged him into it, wrecking his otherwise perfect life. Throwing away twenty-five-years even though he's always been HIV negative. He hates me for ruining his picture-perfect life. He should never have come along on this cruise. It was my mistake. I thought he might show some sympathy and forgive me. I was wrong. He thinks all these promiscuous guys who are like me are the source of the problem, disco airheads fucking strangers at every turn, spreading the virus to good innocent people like himself. I don't know what to do."

The subject was too upsetting to discuss further. I suggested we disembark and explore Rovinj on foot. It's a quaint fishing village with winding cobblestone streets. It's a good distraction with rows of quaint boutiques selling hand painted ceramic plates and mugs to the straight tourists. But after a half hour I wanted to scream. None of these people understood my world. AIDS to them was God's rightful curse on men who dared to do the unspeakable— suck another man's cock and take a hardon up the ass. "Let them all die and go to hell."

I excused myself and walked back to the boat. I was exhausted. I went by the lounge on the upper deck. It was empty. The view back towards Rovinj was lovely with its pastel-colored houses like in a children's picture book. It made me think back on my ex-lover Jim of nine years. Jim preceded Abbey. He was the editor of children's books when we lived in New York City. Jim died of AIDS last year. I miss him. He was a good man, always a true friend. I recalled how Dylan rarely showed Jim any sympathy. That was not right.

As my mind drifted off aimlessly taking in the fishing boats lining the harbor, I noticed someone in my peripheral vision. It was an older white-haired gentleman dressed in chinos and a colored sports shirt with a fancy camera around his neck. He had an open friendly face that I found most comforting in my current state. "May I join you? I have the exact same sport shirt from Cornell. We must both be alumni yes?" "Indeed. I'm Miles. Architecture Class of seventy-four, retired." "I'm Troy, glad to meet you. I was in Landscape Architecture Class of seventy-seven. Now I'm a half-time landscape designer in Dayton, Ohio and half-time Brand Q's official photographer. Would you believe Brand Q actually pays me to take photos of our guests, instant memories; I'm known as the onboard resident shutter bug. I enjoy meeting the guys. Plus the free travel to wonderful places. Brand Q attracts the best and the hottest men."

Just talking to this fellow Troy I felt much better, like my old self again. My morning anxiety vanished. "Troy, I really like you. You send out a positive vibe. I'm traveling with my husband Abbey and our best buddy Toby. If you're free for dinner sometime I'm sure they'd love to meet you; Toby is also a classmate of mine from Cornell." "Sure thing, how about tomorrow Wednesday? The food here in the upper deck lounge is the best on the ship. They open for dinner at five o'clock. Meanwhile let me snap your picture. You never know, you may want it someday. An instant memory. I'll bring along a print to dinner."

That's how I met Troy. A lucky accident. I couldn't wait to tell Abbey and Toby, especially Toby. He could really use a supportive buddy. Dylan was such a drag. Troy seemed like a natural friend— Cornell grad, happy gentleman gardener and an avid world traveler. Troy seemed like a real people person. A lot like Toby and Abbey.

Feeling much better I took a stroll around the upper deck. I ran into our friends from the Pines, Tom and Randy. Tom was busy painting at his easel; the subject was cute guys in skimpy swim suits hanging out in colorful deck chairs. Very sexy. Tom is the leading plein-air painter in the Pines. He usually paints landscapes. He mixed things up for Brand Q. He shows in the respected Fischbach Gallery on 57th street in the city. He's always glad to see me since we share a love of art. Randy looked up from his book, stood up and gave me a hug. Tom and Randy are old lovers. They are inseparable. Randy adores Tom. They love to travel. Tom told me they just got back from Giverny, France tracing the footsteps of Tom's hero Claude Monet. Even though Tom has full blown AIDS, he has more energy than all these dizzy disco queens put together. Tom's an inspiration to us all. I told them Abbey will want to see them. He'll give them a call and set up a dinner date onboard the ship. Maybe we can all go disco dancing afterwards. Tom and Randy's close friends Murry and Richard might want to join us. Plus we want to hear all about Giverny. Our social calendar was already filling up.

# DAY 4, THURSDAY — SIBENIK

Sibenik is famous for the Krka National Park with its wonderland of thundering waterfalls. Toby and Abbey were hot to see it. I decided to call Troy to see if he was up for a private tour. He said sure. He's been there several times. It's super cool. You'll get soaked so dress accordingly, probably a swim suit is best. It was spectacular. Troy took us by boat to the core area where walking trails weave past moss-covered boulders, dozens of waterfalls and pristine soaking pools large for groups and intimate for couples. We watched gay guys having sex in pools. I wanted to strip down and join them. It was like the Garden of Eden. Abbey and I made love under a waterfall. It was like fucking while getting a strong massage at the same time. Toby and Troy disappeared hand-in-hand into a sunny grotto with smooth round boulders all around. I watched Toby butt fuck Troy over a sunny boulder. I had to watch. His gorgeous white butt fucking Toby in the bright sunshine was extremely hot, like my own private porno scene. I knew Toby wouldn't care in the least. I could tell my spying turned both of them on. When Toby was at last finished he turned Troy's torso around and gave him tremendous head. It was beautiful to watch. Afterwards we played tag together in the pools like a bunch of schoolboys. I realized I had just witnessed the birth of a new relationship. Both new lovers were radiant. Toby simply couldn't keep his hands off Troy. It was as if they'd been struck by lightning.

Walking back we traded stories from Cornell, filling in the details of our separate but similar lives. None of us brought up

Dylan. When I disclosed my HIV+ status, Troy didn't hesitate to tell us he was also HIV+. No big deal. I could see Toby was really thankful for my bringing us HIV+ guys together. It means a lot. When Toby shared his sex story from our recent trip to the Fortuny Museum in Venice, I knew he was feeling much better. Troy slapped Toby's beautiful rump hard just once. The loud crisp pop was spectacular. Troy summed it up nicely, "You devil Toby, I'm a lot like you."

The love birds wanted to retire to the privacy of Troy's cabin. Of course we understood. I told them Abbey and I are hosting a dinner party tomorrow in Dubrovnik's best Italian restaurant to celebrate their new relationship. Tom and Randy, plus Murray and Richard want to join us. Perhaps we could all stop off at the Pussy Cat afterwards to burn off some calories disco dancing. Abbey and I are also hot to check out the local sex club next door, The Cock. Nice name.

Before turning in for the night Abbey suggested a night cap at Last Call on the lower deck. I spotted Del in the back corner surrounded by several twinkies. When he saw us he got up immediately and gave us warm hugs. Del is our downstairs neighbor in the Pines Coops. He takes a Brand Q cruise every year. He told us he'd be onboard. I knew he had a single cabin on the lower deck. Being a senior he's always on a tight budget. With two hundred guys onboard it took a while to run into him. Del is almost twice our ages. But I never feel the age difference. He is more kid than senior citizen. Del was born in 1915 and always tells the story of when his mother took him across the Brooklyn Bridge on the day it opened.

Del's broad overview of American homosexuality always fascinates me. He is clearly a little old fashioned, such as in his inability to utter the word AIDS. For Del it is always the "Big A." He tells unbelievable stories from his past, like about his military service during WWII when he was a prison guard watching over young Nazi men. He claims that he'd sneak into their cells at night for hot sex. Or the one about how he fucked a hot young stud sound asleep in his boat in the Pines harbor. I wanted to believe them all.

Del is certainly colorful. He had been a "garmento" working as a traveling salesman crisscrossing the country selling cheap lady's dresses out of his car trunk. He has always lived alone. He adored the previous owner of our Coop unit, the design director for Steelcase, who died young from a massive heart attack. Del treasures the nude photo of the stud which he keeps on his nightstand. It shows the guy lying on his back in Del's bed flaunting an ample semi-erect cock.

Obviously, Del enjoys flirting with the Pines boys. He is very social. He lets you know that David Geffen is a personal friend. But Del is also generous. He always makes sure to introduce us to all the Pines celebrities.

Del has a crush on me. He gives the most terrific neck massage with his incredibly strong hands. He winks to let me know when he's available for a quickie just in case I'm feeling horny. I enjoy the attention. Once I caught Del spying on me nude at the outdoor shower. It was a turn-on since I'm something of an exhibitionist. I'm a big fan of outdoor showers; on Fire Island I have to take two showers a day just to jerk-off after being around all those hot Pines men all the time. So when Del spies on me I make sure he gets the whole show start to finish. Afterwards when we cross paths, he always slaps me on the butt. Seriously, Del is more a father than a lover.

After a final round of beers, Abbey and I said good night. Del obviously had his eye on another young twinkie. Del's more than a bit of a chicken hawk. We invited Del to join us tomorrow for dinner in Dubrovnik. He is close friends with Tom and Randy, as well as Murray and Richard. Perhaps he'd like to join us at the Pussy Cat disco. When I mentioned the sex club The Cock, Del said to definitely count him out. "Twinkies don't hang out in sex clubs. They prefer discotheques."

# DAY 5, FRIDAY — DUBROVNIK

**S**amuel and Kenji announced at breakfast that they are disembarking for good in Dubrovnik. Kenji proposed marriage to Samuel last night. Kenji's filthy rich and everyone knows Samuel is a gold digger. They will settle in Kenji's country villa outside Dubrovnik. They met only ten days ago in Venice while waiting for the Brand Q cruise to depart. They are both disco bunnies. Personally I give the whole thing a month tops. Once Kenji sees the light he'll drop Samuel in a heartbeat.

Dinner at ARKA in Dubrovnik's Old Town was perfect. The nine of us including Del ate outside on the main terrace. Toby and Troy sat at the head of the table. Troy declared in front of everyone that Toby simply knocked him off his feet; true love at first sight. That pronouncement was met with cheers. "He's the love of my life. Thank you Toby sweetheart and thank you Miles for making it happen."

We all walked over to the Pussy Cat discotheque afterwards to burn off some calories dancing. Murray stole the floor. He's a very smooth dancer. He attributes it to years of dancing in the Pines Pavilion. "Those Pines queens really know how to move their butts." Del picked up a cute twinkie who he took back to his cabin on the Jolly Roger. He was glowing.

Abbey and I were hot to check out The Cock next door, Dubrovnik's local sex club. With a name like that I had high expectations. I wasn't disappointed. Tonight is their monthly Hardon Party with lots of kinky leather. A couple of Brand Q guys have wandered over to check it out. In the crowd I spotted Ebony and his boyfriend Mohawk. They were busy putting on a sex show on top of the bar.

Bare chested and wearing only black leather chaps, Ebony was standing showing off the night's prize, his nine-inch hardon straight up with a slight arch, ready for some serious action. Mohawk kept leaning over kissing Ebony's oily tip. First he'd just lick it from the base to the tip with that wicked extremely long skinny tongue. Then he stopped completely and zeroed in on just the tiny urethral opening, that tiny slit at the top of Ebony's beautiful cock. He's obviously done this before. He licks the tiny slit carefully. He works his pointed tongue in ever so slightly, just the very tip. Ebony goes nuts. He starts moaning. I hear heavy breathing. Next thing you know Ebony starts getting antsy. I can see the pressure building in his enormous Black cock. The cock head is getting swollen dripping oily pre-cum, rock hard. Mohawk continues focused, licking the slit undistracted. Ebony starts heaving even louder and then starts shaking as Mohawk grabs the tube of lube for one long pass on Ebony's tool. Black and glistening in the light it is magnificent. Mohawk works the shaft hard with both hands. Arching his back looking up to heaven. Ebony lets out a deeply felt wail, "I'm cumming." Then again louder. Ebony spasms violently, first once, twice, then three times, bursting out loads of cum with each spasm, until the top of the bar is covered in pools of cum.

The place goes crazy. Ebony looks exhausted, his chaps covered in sweat. He collapses on the floor. I rush to get him a glass of water. Mohawk lets out a deafening whistle and pumps his fist in the air. Guys are busy slipping twenties into Mohawk's pink jockstrap as if he had just won Mr. World Atlas. It's all a bit too macho, but I must admit I found it terribly hot. I rub Ebony's smooth Black head and kiss it gently on the top. "You were awesome my Prince."

Downstairs in the basement was the sex den. After that scene upstairs it seemed a little tame. Some action in a sling. Loud slaps on a bare ass and some rough butt fucking. These guys were strictly anal. They looked like tough local fishermen, both straight and gay. They liked to fuck standing up in the back in a pair of convenient showers. No surprise given that they spend all day in very tight quarters on these small fishing boats, butt-to-butt, surrounded by men. Many wore sexy rubber overalls at sea. Back at port under the showers their glistening butts must simply beg for a fuck. Gay or straight, nobody even cares.

Walking back to the Jolly Roger in the cool night air I took Abbey's hand in mine and stopped to give him a slow wet kiss on the mouth. After The Cock I was extremely turned on. I slid my hand inside the back of his Levi's squeezing his warm butt cheeks. Kneeling down Abbey opened my fly and gave me the most wonderful blowjob on the spot. Abbey knows just how to make love to my cock. He's truly my Master.

A young gay couple headed into The Cock saw us and let out a sharp whistle. "You go girls! You're hot." God I love Abbey. I'm such a lucky man. He loves me unconditionally. And I'm a handful. I'm HIV+, damaged goods, but he doesn't care in the least. Of course we always play extra safe. Abbey takes good care of me. He knows our love will see us through.

Thus far the Brand Q cruise has been a great success. Lots of terrific guys. My only disappointment was with Dylan. He was acting out, always so cranky, borderline antisocial. Toby told me he's moved to an empty single cabin. But I really like Troy. He's just what Toby needs after Dylan, a sweet loving guy. I think they'll make a great couple.

# DAY 6, SATURDAY —
# MONOPOLI

One of the unknowns of this Brand Q cruise was today's trip to Monopoli. I hoped to meet my Italian cousin Gerald. My sister tracked down his address from the States. I wrote him and gave him the date I'd be in Monopoli. The note was in English so I wasn't confident I'd connect with anybody. I was in for a real surprise. Not only was my cousin waiting to see me, but it turned out he's gay and he's a screaming drag queen to boot. Gerald is more accurately Geraldine. I mentioned in my English note that I'd be wearing a red I Love NY baseball cap.

As I stepped on land at sunrise I heard this loud shriek, "Miles come to Geraldine sweetie. Come home to Mama." It was most unreal. As I hugged this new stranger I wondered if I had made a huge mistake. Geraldine asked me where my luggage was as if I'd be staying for a month. When she saw Abbey standing at my side she whistled loudly, "Mr. Butch come sit next to Geraldine." Abbey didn't miss a beat. "Think you can handle New York City cock? Be careful or I'm going to have to give you a spanking." It was outrageous, as if we were back in Julius's in the West Village.

Geraldine is out of her closet 100% in Monopoli. She's known as the town's Royal Princess. I sensed she was well loved and respected. I was touched.

Geraldine had arranged an official sunrise breakfast with the town mayor a super-hip lesbian. Monopoli was quite the town. They rolled out the red carpet. Geraldine wore her good pearls. Abbey, Toby, Troy and I met everyone in town worth knowing. Lots of queer jokes and tons of laughter. Thank goodness Troy had his camera. People wouldn't believe it otherwise. We parted with a few tears.

I shared my HIV+ status with Geraldine. She asked and was relieved I was still healthy. I told her about our mutual cousin Sister Sofia in the convent in Venice and her amazing work with PWAs. Geraldine thanked me for the information and will be in touch with Sister Sofia. Maybe something similar could be done at the local hospital here in Monopoli.

As we departed late morning with hugs and tears to board the Jolly Roger, a friendly young priest approached me from out of nowhere. He was really cute. He introduced himself as Father Gerome. He's one of the Catholic priests at the Cathedral Maria Santissima Madia in Monopoli. He's headed to Malta and will be joining us on the Jolly Roger. He's hot to see the Caravaggio paintings in St John's Co-Cathedral in Valletta. He's a Caravaggio groupie like me. In exchange for the passage to Malta he will provide an early morning Catholic Mass on the Jolly Roger each morning. Brand Q has discovered that not surprisingly, these gay cruises attract plenty of conflicted gay Catholics looking for salvation on the dance floor. All that cock sucking and butt fucking all night long requires Father Gerome's blessing the morning after.

I liked Father Gerome immediately. His black robes and white collar made a sharp contrast with all those bare assed hunks in jockstraps. He was obviously gay himself and fit right in with his perfect English. I caught him checking me out more than once. I think he's in the closet.

Meanwhile, I really wanted to do something special for Geraldine after my too brief but wonderful visit. I called up Mrs. J on the Jolly Roger. She's the official Director of Social Activities. I knew she would help. The Jolly Roger doesn't set sail for Saranda until midnight. How about if we put on a drag show tonight in the ship's night club The Stardust? Recreate The Supremes, for one night only. And why not? They were a class act. Everybody loves Motown right? Geraldine could be Diana Ross. She even sounds like her. Geraldine loved the idea. A chance to use all those sequined gowns in her closet. Mrs. J knew that four drag queens were Brand Q passengers in two double rooms on the lower deck. Of course they were thrilled with the assignment.

So Geraldine with her suitcase of gowns joined Father Gerome and me headed back to the Jolly Roger. Mrs. J immediately reserved The Stardust for today and evening and Captain Brook made a general ship-wide announcement. The show would run from nine to midnight with two intermissions, an open bar, tickets going for a hundred dollars each. The Stardust seats a maximum of fifty persons. Jackie offered to handle the ticket sales. It was a very hot item. Jackie sold out in twenty minutes. Troy and Toby offered to oversee the stage lighting including spots for the performers. The "Girls" included Geraldine as Diana Ross, Stephanie as Florence Ballard, Marcia as Mary Wilson and Christina as Betty McGlown. Fortunately they were all traveling with dozens of over-the-top gowns so they'd look the part. Marcia has performed as a Supreme before; so she offered to coach the other girls. Captain Brook told them they had The Stardust starting at 1 o'clock. That would give them eight hours to plan, dress and rehearse. Tight but Geraldine was confident it was all doable. She's been a huge fan of Diana Ross her whole life so knowing the music will be the easy part. The three back-up ladies will need to practice their moves. Mrs. J offered to coach them. She was a little bit jealous actually. Everybody knows drag queens love to perform.

Well amazingly, it all came together at the last minute. Geraldine stole the show. She really had Diana Ross down perfectly. Love Child, You Keep Me Hanging On, Stop! In the Name of Love, You Can't Hurry Love, I Hear A Symphony, Come See About Me, Back In My Arms Again and Baby Love. The boys gave them a warm welcome and ended up giving them all standing ovations. At midnight Geraldine stepped off the Jolly Roger with fresh bouquets of roses and cheers from her adoring new fans.

Afterwards I had a late-night drink and chit-chat with Father Gerome at Last Call. He has a church service on the Main deck first thing in the morning. I think he has the hots for me. He was playing footsie under the table the whole time. I think he was hoping to get inside my pants tonight when Abbey wasn't around. I'll have to make extra sure he meets Abbey in the morning. I'll make sure to introduce him as my husband. I guess he thinks that since it's a gay cruise he can hit on anyone onboard. We're all off sightseeing in Saranda in the morning with Troy as our host. I hope it goes well.

I got up early to attend Father Gerome's Sunday church service. It was a nice change from the disco. Afterwards Troy has volunteered to take Father Gerome, Toby, Abbey and I on a day trip to see the remains of a Roman city at Saranda. Troy actually just wanted to show off his extensive knowledge of sustainable urban planning to his new beau Toby. He's both an urban planner and a landscape architect. I was probably the only one onboard actually interested in such an esoteric topic. Toby of course just wanted to be near his new heart throb Troy. You can tell they are deeply in love. Father Gerome, the queer wandering priest, is interested in all things Roman. And everybody except Father Gerome knows that Abbey and I always do everything together. "Father Gerome, I'm not sure you've met Abbey yet. He's my sweetheart husband."

The Roman city was an early example of site planning that preserved precious resources and essential water to support both agriculture and elaborate baths for all its citizens. The baths were used for bathing as well as sexual pleasure in a complex of steam rooms and cold chambers. Ancient Romans always held homosexual pleasure between elders and young boys in the highest regard. It was their way of passing life experience and knowledge from one generation to the next.

It all sounded so wonderful. I felt like I'd been cheated. We all did. Troy showed us the private walled quarters of Emperor Hadrian and his lover Antinous. An island in a giant pool with huge gold fish, it had retractable wooden bridges to insure privacy for the couple during the heat of anal sex. Obviously Hadrian was the top,

Antinous was the bottom. It must have been super-hot. You can see erotic frescoes depicting all of this and more in the Gabinetto Segreto, or Secret Cabinet in the National Archaeological Museum of Naples. Sorry our cruise doesn't include a stop there.

Back onboard the Jolly Roger we took a nap followed by a simple light dinner. Tonight is the infamous Black Party, a must see in all the gay guide books. The Lost Boys will be out tonight for sure. Plenty of cock and ass. The main deck was turned into an orgy den with guys fucking out in the open, raw and raunchy. Mac and Ray were out of their cabin for the first time in days. Mac wouldn't miss this scene for the world. Ebony and Mohawk were busy performing continuous live sex acts on a raised platform for hours. It was incredible. We simply watched from the sidelines. By evening's end the deck floor was covered in used condoms, pools of spent cum everywhere.

Dylan made a late brief appearance. He was alone and barely spoke to anyone. When he saw Toby and Troy dancing together he approached Toby. "Well aren't you going to introduce me to your new boyfriend?" Toby hesitated a long couple of seconds. "I'm not sure what the point is Dylan, since he's HIV positive. You don't approve of guys who happen to be positive." Dylan was speechless and walked away without another word.

The morning cleanup crew in their pristine white outfits will have their work cut out for themselves. That is unless hungry sea gulls don't first go mad feasting on the glaze of cock semen. Probably best to flush the whole deck down with plenty of water using the fire hoses.

# DAY 8,
# MONDAY — GALLIPOLI, PUGLIA

I was up early. The sky was pink tinged with robin egg blue, that pretty pale blue green that Tiffany & Co. uses on all their gift boxes. Abbey always insists we keep those boxes to recycle at a later date. They are special with special memories. As I strolled the upper main promenade I watched the small army of Brand Q maintenance guys in their white overalls and white gloves, their fancy mini-vacs that were so quiet I always thought they were turned off. They were busy sucking up hundreds of used condoms from last night's revelers. I'd see rubbers everywhere, in hidden hallways, outer decks and the back stairs. All places where men had had passionate sex, whether it be out in the open as shameless exhibitionists or tucked away in hidden corners so your husband won't stumble upon your infidelity.

I paused at the main deck to watch Father Gerome's eight o'clock Catholic Mass. It must have broken all attendance records. It was actually crowded. It was obviously a public show of guilt following the raunchy Black Party the night before. Now guys were saying prayers on the same site where they were screwing just a few hours ago. Morally conflicted guys who practice Catholicism in the dining room while fucking by night in the disco; trying to have things both ways. They wanted to cleanse their bodies, to cleanse their very souls. Only time will heal the wounds. Father Gerome's morning-after-prayers were pretty worthless. What's done is done.

The Forgiveness Mass over, Father Gerome joined Abbey and I, plus Toby and Troy for an outing to picturesque Gallipoli. The historic Old Town is an island off the mainland reached by an ancient bridge. First stop was lunch at Osteria Briganti famous for their daily fresh fish.

Strolling the crooked streets of Old Town afterwards, Abbey spotted a rainbow flag hanging from an open second floor window. A shirtless body builder was posing at the window. He was in spandex gym trunks that revealed everything. He smiled. Abbey told me he was a cock tease. He was too bold. Abbey was right. When we passed his window on the return walk he was still there but the flag was gone. This time around the show was all for a group of young horny ladies.

We headed for the remote gay beach mentioned in the guide book. A little sun and fun. Toby and Troy found a secluded private cove for lovemaking. Father Gerome was nervous. I could tell he really wanted to make things right between the three of us. "Please forgive me fellas. Last night I was really out of line Miles. I'm sorry. I drank too much. I really love you guys. I hope we can still be friends." I was touched. I knew sex had the power to make things right. "How about giving Abbey and me blow jobs, one at a time, taking turns out in the open? That could be therapeutic." "I would like to. I'd be honored." Father Gerome was a highly skilled cocksman. After that long session he can blow us anytime he wants. Abbey called him Father, I called him just Gerome. I liked that more. It sounded like a sex buddy. I asked him to keep the white collar on the whole time. I have a thing for white collars. My priest back in Albuquerque always blew me with his white collar on. Gerome liked the idea. To wrap things up we double-teamed Father Gerome with a two-handed jerkoff session. I could tell he really enjoyed that. We were finally best friends. Just a little queer sex between us made everything right. Afterwards a dip in the ocean with a group hug. We all walked back slowly to the Jolly Roger feeling closer than ever. We were really bonding. Father Gerome opened up declaring his love for each of us. Suddenly he felt part of our family. I told him I loved him.

At the bridge to Old Town we saw Mr. Rainbow Flag posing against the bridge railing like a seasoned street hustler with a raised knee. He must be bisexual covering all the bases. He smiled for us. He was quite handsome up close. I guess business was slow. It must be rough. Gallipoli is not exactly Times Square.

Toby and Troy said good night early. They are still in their honeymoon phase with sex at least twice a day. First Toby approached Father Gerome privately about Dylan. He asked him to check in on him occasionally. "He could use a friend." Father Gerome said he would gladly drop in on Dylan tomorrow. Maybe he's available for dinner.

Abbey pulled me aside. He's hot for that promised second tour of the ship's engine room. I'm more interested in Pedro's white work overalls and his sexy white butt. Well of course we ended up with both. We took turns butt fucking the kid. He's strictly a bottom which suited us both fine. He dropped the overalls and leaned over the padded workbench. It was really hot with the sound of the giant well-oiled ship pistons going in the background. Pedro suggested we use a few drops of pure motor oil for our sex lube. He does that all the time. It was fantastic. A super-smooth ride.

# DAY 9, TUESDAY — AT SEA

I was up early. Our next destination was Syracuse. It's twice our usual overnight travel distance aboard the Jolly Roger, so we'll be at sea the entire day. Fine with me. I crave a serious workout at the gym. It's been over a week. I'm long overdue. I miss that post-gym burn of my muscles. It makes me feel alive. Abbey thinks I'm a little crazy. He spends only half the time I do in the gym. It's also the camaraderie I crave, working out next to friendly sexy guys. Spotting for each other, pushing each other on with that extra set you didn't think you had in you.

The Jolly Roger had a serious gym. A full circuit of strength training machines and a huge selection of bikes and treadmills to burn off those calories. I did an hour on the bike before hitting the free weights. The guy working out next to me was super-friendly and asked me if I needed a spot. "Sure. I always push myself more with a gym buddy. Hi I'm Miles." "Great, I'm Greg." Greg was a Texan from Dallas. He had an adorable Texan drawl and a Texan basket to go with it. We shared an obsession with six-pack abs. He had a gorgeous set that looked like those I'd seen on Chippendale dancers in porno flicks. Greg was modest about it. He kept his tank top on the whole time. He gave me a few tips to help me bring out muscle definition. By the time our session was over my muscles were aching with that deep burn I always crave.

Time to hit the steam room. The workout left me horny. I was disappointed when Greg declined my invitation. I had hoped to lick his abs. No such luck. Greg was off with a goodbye to find his boyfriend for a jog around the upper deck. I knew Abbey would still be sleeping so I decided to hit the hot tub for a little soak in my Speedos. I had a pleasant surprise. Ebony was in the water all by himself. He nodded as I got in next to him. God were his baby blues beautiful. He was also in his white Speedos. I could easily make out his semi-erect cock inside the skimpy trunks. He saw me staring and slipped them off. I followed suit. Soon his tool looked just like what I remembered from the Hardon Party at The Cock. Nine-inches hard straight up with a slight arch. I smiled. "You sure have a beautiful tool. Want some head?" "Sure, but I really owe you. That night at The Cock you were the guy who gave me a glass of water when I really needed it. Let me thank you properly. Want to fuck me in the steam room? White guys always say they love to fuck me." Without waiting for my answer he stood up and sashayed across the deck into the steam room. What a butt crack on this guy. I was hooked. I followed him immediately.

The steam was super-thick. I couldn't see a damn thing. I picked up a condom from the Brand Q dispenser inside the door. Slowly moving towards the back I could just barely make out Ebony. He was leaning over a bench waiting patiently. For the first time I could really appreciate his gorgeous Black body. What a gift. As my cock slid up his tight butthole I moaned softly in total pleasure. What an erotic sight. I always dream of this, my white hardon sliding up some stud's beautiful Black butt. Ebony pushed back firmly taking each thrust in deep. When I finally burst my load, he yelled out and slapped my butt cheeks hard. What a beautiful Black lover. "Thank you brother. You're my Prince." I'd never forget our brief encounter.

When I caught up with Abbey back at our cabin he wanted all the details. I told him everything. He hugged me and affectionately called me "My Stud." Abbey's great that way. He always gives me total space. He's never judgmental. Which means I can be a hundred percent honest with him in return. We are completely in love.

In the afternoon Abbey and I played a game of Scrabble in the upper deck lounge with Murray and Richard. I'm a decent player, but Abbey always wins. He learned to play from his mom Shirley who was a real champion. She never cheated using a dictionary and she knew all those two and three letter words that always come in handy. Richard is a serious player as well, but Abbey squeaked out a win just barely with the word "nauseous."

We shared a pizza around the time the piano bar kicked in.

It drew a dozen guys including Dylan and Father Gerome who is seriously into English musicals. He was soon red in the face. He sang with great gusto, his arms flailing constantly in all directions as if he was Leonard Bernstein conducting the New York Philharmonic. Richard called for time out and sang a powerful rendition of "Nessun Dorma" from Puccini's opera Turandot. "Let no one sleep." That brought down the house. Everyone went nuts. Richard sings regularly with an amateur opera company in Brooklyn not far from where Murray and Richard live. Richard sings Puccini arias in the house all day long. His dad from Sicily brought up Richard on opera starting in the crib. Richard and Murray's adopted son Seth also caught the opera bug, that plus a personal interest in street rap. Seth's a Mr. Cool street rapper.

In the crowded room I noticed Dylan seated in a corner. He was probably waiting for Father Gerome for their dinner date. Father Gerome who was playing the piano finally noticed Dylan. He stopped abruptly and they disappeared down the stair to the middle deck. Dylan looked glad to see him. Later I mentioned this to Abbey. He'll check in tomorrow with Father Gerome; give us the latest scoop on Dylan. Abbey was relieved.

For just a simple day at sea I was exhausted. Abbey had a night cap with Murray and Richard. I turned in. The full moon's reflection off the waves was eerie. It reminded me of those creepy paintings by Edvard Munch.

# DAY 10, WEDNESDAY — SYRACUSE

I woke up extra early. It was still dark out. The full moon was still out from the night before. It was now low on the horizon. It was like a vision out of a dream. Abbey was still sound asleep. We always sleep in the nude. I like to take advantage of the situation. I start rubbing his back. Abbey loves that. It takes him back to his childhood. He always starts moaning softly. As I focus in on his warm butt, he moans louder. As my fingers work his gorgeous butt crack, he pushes his ass tight against me. By that point my cock is already hard and wet. I start rimming him. I could do that forever. A touch of lube, I gently work in a pair of fingers real slow. "Go ahead Miles fuck me." I slip it in. Abbey knows me so well. He pushes back. That's how I make love to my sweetheart Abbey, my prince, as the sun breaks. My cock is deep up his beautiful hot butt. We are together in heaven.

We took a quick rinse together. After our morning sex I felt like an early dawn run around the middle deck. Abbey went back to sleep. It's dead quiet. I seem to have the ship to myself. The morning rays are just breaking. It's extremely beautiful. As I take in the golden sunlight glancing off the broadside of the ship I admire its steel superstructure, an engineer's work of art. It's a very rational structure, a delicate web of posts and cable railings shimmering in the sunlight.

That's when I first noticed the rope, a thin soft sailing rope, white with red stripes. It appeared to be tied to an outer railing low to the floor, barely visible, running down the side of the ship at an angle, then out of sight. As I leaned forward I could just barely make out a body hanging free far below, swaying in the breeze. I was stunned. The rope was tied tight around the figure's neck. My first instinct was to pull on the rope, hoist the body back on board, rescue him. Then I recognized the figure's sweater. It was a red and white Cornell letter sweater. It was Dylan's sweater. I'd seen it a hundred times. I knew then all was lost. Dylan had hung himself. He was dead. I felt sick, as if I might vomit. I panicked. There was nothing to do. I was too late. Dylan must have been swinging from that rope for hours. In the moonlight while I was making love to Abbey in the safety of our bed, Dylan was battling his demons in the night where in desperation he must have drunk half a gallon of vodka, fixed the rope around his neck with the sailor's knot he knew so well, then hurled himself overboard, flying briefly in the briefest escape, before the sharp single jolt snapped his neck clean in an instant, dead in an instant, to swing for hours unnoticed in the moonlight. Only I alone half understood what had happened.

The rest was a blur. Loud pounding on Captain Brook's door. He immediately sent out a Morse code. Poor Jackie collapsed on the floor in tears upon hearing the news. Brook laid out Dylan's body on the main deck under a sheet of plastic and blankets. He rushed to Dylan's single cabin looking for clues. Sure enough Dylan had left a sealed envelope on the desk with Brook's name on it. Its contents clarified little. As in life, Dylan revealed little in death. Just a request to Captain Brook for a Burial at Sea in a simple pine box. Father Gerome showed up sheepishly most upset, racked with guilt. He had been the last person on the ship to spend time with Dylan. Why hadn't he been more observant? In spite of that he managed to perform a makeshift blessing over the body with a small bouquet of tired flowers from the kitchen. He was in tears. Obviously it was too late to administer last rights. Toby looked on from the sidelines, grim, in complete shock. Troy stood by protectively enfolding Toby in his arms.

The phone call to Grinnell, Iowa was the most difficult. Dylan had never come out to his family so Toby was treated as nonfamily in spite of the twenty-five years of living with Dylan. His sister, first hysterical in disbelief, came around to full agreement for a Burial at Sea in a plain box per Dylan's written request. She backed off when Toby and Troy offered to pay all funeral expenses. The hastily arranged ceremony by Captain Brook was stiff and uninspired. Dylan would have been appalled. I was overlooked and completely ignored. Rumor spread that Toby and Troy discovered the body first, not me. Who really cares?

I was exhausted. I took a nap. When I woke up at noon I was so relieved that we seemed to be through the worst of it. Hopefully it would all be over today. This is our last full day on the Jolly Roger. Tonight is the long scheduled White Party. Given last night's ordeal guys thought that was inappropriate. Even those who never knew Dylan felt odd. The Captain made an announcement mid-afternoon that this evening's White Party would go on but it would be treated as a memorial service honoring Dylan. He asked everyone to dress appropriately and behave themselves. No disco music, Dylan would have preferred Puccini. "Please show Dylan your respect." It was a beautiful event and all the more moving since this was the last night of our cruise together; we'd be disembarking in Malta tomorrow at noon. The most touching moment came when Toby spoke in front of everyone paying tribute to the twenty-five years he and Dylan had shared living together. He told many touching and funny stories from their travels, like the time the guard locked Dylan up inside the Great Pyramid of Giza. Or at the Louvre in Paris when Dylan called a female guard "cunt face" and had to be escorted out of the museum leaving Toby behind. That was pure Dylan. Afterwards there was lots of slow dancing with couples wrapped up in each other's arms. There was more conversation than normal. Guys chose their best dress shorts over jockstraps. Everyone wanted to give Toby a hug. He was able to finally forgive Dylan for his years of blame and anger over Toby's HIV status. Everyone joined in a heartfelt toast to Toby and Troy.

# DAY 11,
# THURSDAY — VALETTA,
# MALTA

Abbey and I arranged a farewell breakfast in Valetta with Toby and Troy, Mac and Ray, Murray and Richard, Tom and Randy. Toby announced he is going to Dayton, Ohio with Troy. He will try his hand at a little gardening and landscape architecture. They are all excited, completely in love. Hugs all around. Murray and Richard will be off shortly picking up the kids Seth and Sophie in Verona on the way to Rome. Murray's mom is staying behind. She fell in love with Verona and announced her plans to move there permanently. I was not terribly surprised.

Abbey and I joined up with Father Gerome for our pilgrimage to Caravaggio's masterpiece, The Beheading of Saint John the Baptist. It's in the Oratory of St. John's Co-Cathedral in Valletta. It's enormous at twelve by seventeen feet, the artist's largest work. The half dozen figures depicted are painted full life-size surrounded by Caravaggio's signature sea of darkness. We were overwhelmed.

It was a little too close to last night's events for comfort. Death and human cruelty are laid out bare in the monumental canvas. The martyred saint is on the ground bleeding heavily, his head still partially attached as the executioner over him pulls out a small hand knife to finish the messy job. The jailer with keys points to the platter which Salome lowers to receive the severed head. The scene is cold and very matter-of-fact, a messy gruesome job, inhumane at best. Only the old woman in the back clasping her head in her hands appears to be moved by the horrific scene. There are no angels waiting in the wings. No divine light streams down from heaven.

Where a halo would normally hang over a saint's head is found only the executioner's hand gripping the Baptist's hair to complete Harod's merciless order. Caravaggio spares the viewer nothing. It is pure distilled Caravaggio at his best.

Staring up at the painting seated I asked myself why does Caravaggio have such a powerful hold on us gays? It's more than the skimpily clad youths, the guards in black leather. We all secretly admire and envy his eccentric and violent life. It's well documented in the police records of his time, his duels, the murder, fleeing Rome for his life, joining the Knights of Malta, a mysterious all-male club. Then his insulting a superior, his hot-headed tirades, jailed again and an escape. Finally receiving a papal pardon and dying of a malignant fever while attempting to return to Rome, but too late to make things right.

Caravaggio was a homosexual, a street brawler, an ill-tempered quarrelsome genius who was both envious and proud, jealous and vain. His brilliant paintings were highly contentious in his day, placing the downtrodden poor, the dirty laborer, the unfaithful sinner on center stage on the high altar. We secretly adore this brave queer hero whose self-portrait lives forever in the dark corners of his paintings bearing witness to their infidelities, their betrayals, their silent horrors.

Our Brand Q cruise is over. We parted company with Father Gerome wishing him all the best. He's a new friend. We'll stay in touch. He's taking the bus back to Monopoli. It's not hard to imagine him living in such a small magical town. Abbey and I have planned a three-day stay in Rome before returning to Albuquerque. We'll spend the night in Valetta and then catch the first Frecciarossa train to Rome in the morning. It's Italy's high-speed train; it reaches a speed of 250 miles per hour.

# DAY 12, FRIDAY — GETTING KINKY

Our taxi driver from the Rome train station dropped us off at Largo dei Librari in front of our four-story mustard-colored apartment building. Everything looked the same as we had left it ten months prior. The schoolchildren were still smoking under the white umbrellas at the Tabacchi, the cobblestones were still a little dirty, but the doll-house façade of our tiny church Santa Barbara looked different. The once gray façade of our charming church had been cleaned to a soft glowing cream in our absence. At ten that morning, the outdoor café was already busy. We needed to kill a few hours while waiting for the cleaning crew to finish a pass through our apartment. No problem, Largo dei Librari felt like our second home.

Abbey decided to have an espresso. I felt like a caffe latte. We settled in and ordered. Everything was delicious as usual. I glanced at the two middle-aged women at the next table speaking in German quite loudly. Italians rarely, if ever, speak so loudly in public. That's when I noticed that the lady facing me had a remarkable resemblance to our friend Tina, our travel companion from last year. What a surprise.

"So you thought you wouldn't have to put up with me this time around, didn't you?" She sounded just like Margaret Hamilton, the Wicked Witch of the West in The Wizard of Oz.

I bolted out of my chair. I needed to go for a walk. The front door of Santa Barbara beckoned. The door was locked. Then I remembered the church is only open on the weekends. It's Friday. I ducked into Da Vinci on the corner, my favorite men's clothing shop in Rome. The sexy clerk Gino will save me. He knows me well. He likes me. Over the years, I'd spent hours in the shop trying on tight-fitting Italian trousers. But no, this morning, only his mother Loretta was in the shop. Gino had to run to Rome's Motor Vehicle Department. I was doomed.

Leaving the shop crestfallen, I rejoined Abbey at our table. Thank God, the pair of German ladies were gone. Their replacements looked like a gay Italian couple in skin-tight jeans and distressed leather jackets. I immediately tuned in with a nod. The cute short one gave me the careful once over with a friendly smile. "Hi, I'm Rudolfo. How's the espresso here?" "Ask my lover Abbey. He drinks the strong stuff. I'm a caffe latte guy. Ciao! I'm Miles. We just arrived." "Welcome to Roma. I'm Piero. Where are you guys staying?" "Right here, number seventy-eight. The maid is cleaning our apartment. She'll be done by noon." "Cool, maybe we can see more of you guys later." "We sure hope so. Just buzz the bell Branzini, any time after two. Maybe you can help us get over our jet lag." Rudolfo smiled immediately. Piero offered to give each of us a massage later. I'd say we can count on these two for some hot fun.

Tina's ghost witnessed the whole pickup scene. I didn't see her, but I heard her voice clearly inside my head. "You two look like you're up to your old tricks again. Well, play safe. I'll check in later. I miss you."

At four o'clock the door buzzer sounded. I took the elevator down to welcome our new friends in. The tiny cab is meant for just two persons, so we were packed in as tight as sardines. No problem. Sometimes tighter is better. The three of us headed up. "Sorry, I'm still in my gym clothes. I was unpacking." Actually, I had changed into my favorite yellow jockstrap and an old white tank top on purpose. Rudolfo noticed. He gave the swollen yellow pouch a gentle squeeze with one hand as he slid a finger of his other hand up and down my exposed butt crack. I gave him a smile. "Thanks Rudolfo, that feels exactly like what I need." Abbey was waiting for us inside in his skimpy gym shorts. Piero knelt down immediately without saying a word and started blowing him in the living room. I handed Rudolfo a fresh condom. "Go ahead, you want to fuck me right? I can see your beautiful Italian cock is rock hard. Please fuck me with your leather jacket on. I was admiring it in the square. It looks super-hot. I think I'll also leave my jockstrap on if you don't mind. I'd really like that." "We think alike. I think you Americans call it 'kinky.'" "Yea, you got that right. Let's get down to it kinky. Let's start by letting me rim your pretty butt."

We had kinky sex that afternoon, taking turns trading positions. Piero and Rudolfo were highly skilled cocksmen. They were also insatiable and hung like a pair of Italian stallions. Afterwards, we had thin-crust Roman pizzas downstairs in the square while we traded stories of Rome and New York City. Rudolfo told me where to look for a vintage leather jacket. There's a great small vintage clothing shop just around the corner. The owner is gay. His name is Claudio. He's a sweetheart.

Our kinky sex left me hornier than ever. Abbey suggested we walk over to Piazza Navona to reacquaint ourselves with Bernini's spectacular fountain, the Fountain of the Four Rivers. A very sexy workman was seated at one of the stone benches. He was clearly cruising me biting his lip. I was hooked in an instant. He was rough and dirty. I liked that. Just what I always crave. Beard stubble from a few days ago. He can see I am interested in him.

He stands up and walks over to Madonna del Sacro Cuore, a minor overlooked church with a back door onto the square. The door is ajar. He enters, we follow. The empty interior is dark and gloomy. I've been here before. It's always deserted. I hear a soft cough in the shadows. He is seated in the back of the first side chapel; he's cloaked in darkness. He's waiting patiently for me to place my hardon in his hungry mouth. As I approach next to him, he impulsively takes hold of my jeans, ripping the button fly open, taking my entire hardon into his mouth in one pass, deep down into his throat. He's a master cocksucker. I'm in for a treat.

He's hungry, slurping saliva all over my cock with his large tongue, the overflow dripping into a pool of saliva on the stone floor. I place my hands on his facial cheeks. His beard stubble is even rougher than I had imagined. I rub the individual stiff hairs. They are coarse like a heavy scrub brush. I work them firmly with my fingers, then pause to slide my hardon into his warm wet mouth, pressing the juicy cock deep into his throat. He takes it all, no problem.

This horny stranger will be my Mr. Deep Throat. I consciously decide I will feed him my most precious gift, my fresh cum; he's to feast on every drop. He swallows the cock whole. He works each precious centimeter, base to tip, over and over. Finally my cock pours out its jisim in waves. The release is a flood like a summer's sudden downpour. His obedient tongue takes it all in, not missing a single drop. We both chuckle like naughty schoolboys. I kiss the top of his head. I'm completely drained, his feasting is over. I rebutton my fly and walk out of the darkness into the brilliant late-afternoon sun.

Across the piazza Bernini's naked river gods greet Abbey and I with their beefy butts, their massive backsides. I'm no longer interested in Bernini. Rather I fondly replay the mental tapes of my dirty workman. His rough beard stubble, my cock down his throat dripping saliva, his powerful tongue working my shiny shaft. I already crave his rough touch. I know I will never see him again. We were two outlaws lusting after the same thing, male-to-male contact.

# DAY 13,
## SATURDAY — SANTA BARBARA

iny Santa Barbara had been closed for days. Then I noticed the front door was open at nine o'clock on a Saturday morning. We spotted the open door from our third-floor windows overlooking the quaint church square. Abbey spends hours at the windows looking down at the urban scene below; schoolchildren playing, café loungers gossiping, shoppers resting, the African street musician singing softly.

At the square's center sits the tiny church. The saint's statue is placed high on the facade gazing down on the square below. Barbara is holding the palm of martyrdom standing before a fortified tower. The saint's legend alleges her pagan father kept her locked up in a tower before having her martyred, as a result of which she was struck by lightning. At her feet are two tiny cannons, back-to-back, shooting out fire and lightning bolts. Barbara is still Rome's patron saint of firefighters. Many assume Santa Barbara is Rome's smallest church, but with over nine-hundred churches in the Eternal City, who knows for sure. She presents a modest 17th century baroque facade, more a doll's house than a Roman monument, its two stories more classical than high baroque, by the little-known architect Giuseppe Passeri. It's limestone facade sits quietly between the mustard, orange and honey-colored buildings.

Roman churches always offer a welcome escape. Their often empty, cool stone interiors provide an immediate break with the bustling over-heated city in which they are embedded. Passing through the wooden vestibule into Santa Barbara, I sense a magician's hand as I'm transported to another time, another universe all together. The church is a Greek cross in plan conceived as four equal arms around a heavenly dome. It is a reference to ancient Byzantium, an abstract geometric perfection that places humankind at its center.

The small church interior is a feast of pastel faux colored marbles. Just inside the dimly lit interior a large tryptic greets me: Madonna and Child, flanked by John the Baptist and a youthful Archangel Michael. Instantly the old familiar stories return in a jumble of blurred fragments, familiar yet vague, soothing in their mystery, but still meaningless.

There is a queer undercurrent here. The only occupant other than me is always the handsome young Catholic priest. He is the sole caretaker who is busy arranging and rearranging the main altar with its flowers and candles. It must be perfect. I have seen him often. He never wears the traditional black robes. Rather he is in black Levi 501s like some street hustler on Christopher Street back in the West Village. As he faces the altar I always enjoy the view of his plump butt in skin-tight jeans. I swear he has to be gay. I can easily imagine the two of us in a sex scene in the vestry, all hot and flustered, raw and raunchy, but I always restrain myself. Instead I offer him a harmless adoring smile. He always smiles back.

In the adjacent side chapel, a large 14th century wooden crucifix holds a tired but peaceful life-size body of Christ. He is looking down lovingly, accepting his painful fate. Christ's poignant blessing is meant for both of us equally, two sinners from two different worlds, a wayward young Catholic priest and an adoring lustful acolyte.

# DAY 14, SUNDAY — SANTA MARIA MAGGIORE

I was long overdue for a proper confession in a Roman Catholic Church. Perhaps even a proper spanking given all those mortal sins. After a week aboard the Jolly Roger I had racked up quite a few. The list was too long to recall accurately. Mostly blowjobs. Whatever one imagined it was incomplete. They were all sins of the flesh. Sins which I don't consider sins at all, but rather prayers of adoration, lustful obsessions perhaps, but loving and joyful as well, celebrations of God's divine beauty. First dear Giuseppe at the Danieli, then two visits to his sweet brother Pedro in the engine room on the Jolly Roger. Then kinky Mr. Ebony my obsession. First lusting over him at The Cock, then a private butt fucking session in the steam room that was out of this world. Lastly the blowjobs from Father Gerome for Abbey and I on the beach in Gallipoli. But surely those shouldn't count since he is a practicing Roman Catholic priest. Quite the record for just one week.

I figured I'm in Rome with some spectacular churches, so it was now or never for that overdue confession. Abbey and I wanted to revisit Santa Maria Maggiore anyway. After Saint Peter's in the Vatican it's the most visited Catholic church in all of Rome. High Mass at twelve noon Sunday at Santa Maria Maggiore, that's our ticket. It's over-the-top. Thundering organ music filled the enormous Roman basilica with its splendid mosaics dating back to the year four hundred. A singular strong male voice filled the space, washing over the crowd of pilgrims from across the globe.

I wandered in the empty side aisles peeking into Michelangelo's

Sforza Chapel, Cappella Sistina and the sumptuous Borghese Chapel where a distant namesake, Ludovico Cardi Cigoli, painted frescos over four hundred years ago. I stopped briefly at Bernini's pathetically modest tomb, a mere stone step with his name on it above the family crest. How ironic that a major artistic genius could be so thoughtlessly overlooked in death.

I was struck at the line of wooden confessionals that lined the perimeter walls. There were dozens of them. Nothing like the confessionals of my childhood. Those afforded welcome privacy, a curtain, a door, darkness, a hidden chamber in which to reveal guarded secrets, shameful acts described in whispers, confessed through a sliding screen window.

I was stunned. These confessionals hid nothing. Priest, sinner and sins were all exposed, visible, even audible. Then I thought why not? Maybe this is a better way to deal with sins, especially sins of the flesh. Get them out in the open. That suited my perverted mind fine. Retelling each sin was a turn on. Sharing the details with a stranger priest was erotic. The exhibitionist in me liked the idea. I was soon fully aroused.

I spotted the confessional with the English sign posted over the door; the priest kneeling out front was young, his head shaved, his beard tightly cropped. He looked just like the clerk at the sex shop in the Village back home. He was hot. As I kneeled down right next to him I smiled. He smiled back briefly checking me over. I slid over slightly closer so he could follow my whispers, the hushed language of sex between men.

"Bless me Father for I have had queer sins of the flesh multiple times over the past week, many times more since my last confession." "Tell me all my Son." I described the seven blowjobs one-by-one in great detail. He didn't rush me but took in each word carefully as I whispered the blasphemies out loud one at a time. When I told him how much I enjoyed each encounter he smiled, then chuckled, and asked me for more details. He looked around concerned someone might overhear us. "Hush, hush my Son. Come with me." He took me to a small room off the vestry. He locked the door and then he removed his black robes. He had a tight wrestler's body. He was naked except for an old jockstrap over his beautiful white rump. I left the jockstrap on the whole time. I could tell he really liked that as much as I did. "I'm Miles. What's your name Father?" "I'm Marco." He turned to face the wall with his arms fully outstretched. "Fuck me hard Miles. That is your penance. Fuck me hard Miles."

So first I slapped Marco's butt cheeks hard with my bare hands. "Harder Miles." His hot butt turned bright red. Then I fingered the deep butt crack using plenty of saliva. He moaned audibly. Since he obviously liked that so much, I rimmed his tender anus slowly over and over. I took my time. Well, he moaned even louder. "Go ahead Miles fuck me deep with your big American dick." I slipped on a condom and gave him everything he asked for. He easily took it all in. He was one horny Roman Catholic priest. When it was all over he turned to hug me warmly. Then he blessed me with a sign of the cross on my forehead. "Go in peace my Son. You should come for confession more often. I would love to hear your confession any time in private. God gave you a beautiful cock." We parted with a hug. I will have to write Father Gerome about the whole experience. Maybe he and Father Marco could hook up sometime.

Abbey was waiting for me in a pew nearby the whole time; he'd been following us each step of the way. He's Jewish so Roman Catholic confession doesn't have the same hold on him that it has on me. "You Catholics are sure fucked up when it comes to sex. You're all delusional. But I guess you had a good time right?" "You bet I did, Father Marco was the best. He's a new friend."

After that carnal indulgence we were about to have the most cerebral experience imaginable. Murray and Richard called out of the blue. They are in Rome for several days with Richard's opera friend who's a member of the chorus of Roma's Teatro Opera. He pulled some strings and has arranged for Richard to join the chorus on stage for tonight's performance of Wagner's Pilgrim's Chorus from Tannhauser. Quite an honor. Murray has tickets for his mom, Richard's parents, himself and the kids plus Abbey and I. It's a generous general thank you for the Brand Q cruise. You can imagine Richard is flying like a kite. It's his wildest dream to sing live from the stage of the Teatro Opera in Rome. Richard's Dad is taking everyone out afterwards to celebrate at La Matriciana. He's extremely proud of Richard. The performance came off perfectly. Richard has an open invitation to join the chorus next time he's in Rome.

# DAY 15,
# MONDAY — HEADED HOME

**B**ack on the Alitalia flight home to the Big Apple I felt completely content. We splurged on first class seats at the last moment. We deserved them after such a stressful trip. The Brand Q cruise was still too close to process completely. We needed a little distance to put it in perspective. Despite Dylan's gruesome death I felt wonderful. Even that shock was a positive release, an end to a festering wound. Toby could finally move on. I was grateful for that ironic outcome.

My seatmate Alfonso was a shy young Italian fellow from Genoa, obviously gay, a graphic designer. His first trip to America. So full of potential and promise. We chatted the whole trip. In typical Italian fashion he spoke using his hands constantly. He didn't know how long he'd stay, whether for just a week or a year. I admired his brave attitude, so open-ended. That's how we should all live, on the edge, day to day. He asked me what to see in New York City. I recommended the High Line. Everybody loves it. It allows one to float over the city, to disengage, to escape if only for a few minutes. The city is really unlivable. To say otherwise is a white lie. We're all delusional to choose to live there.

As we parted in the baggage claim area, Abbey and I handed Alfonso our joint card with a pair of warm hugs. Play safe. Alfonso would end up staying in New York City after all. My Cornell friend David, the graphic designer, would end up offering Alfonso a job. Life is a circle. Alfonso would open a satellite graphic design office in Rome.

Troy called from Dayton, Ohio. Toby died before Christmas. He had gone completely blind. He passed away at home in Dayton in Troy's arms. Toby requested no formal service, just a small gathering of friends from the Pines. On a Sunday morning we tossed Toby's ashes into the Atlantic. The sun was shining. I told Sister Sofia of Toby's passing. In his will Toby left everything to the orphanage at the Ospedale Dela Pieta in Venice. Sofia planted an olive tree in the convent's courtyard with a bronze plaque honoring Toby and Troy.

Troy will return to Brand Q in the spring for "the best and the hottest men." This time around it's a twelve-day Egypt Nile River cruise. Toby would approve. Troy is still Brand Q's official photographer, the maker of instant memories.

Captain Brook and Jackie will be onboard.

www.ingramcontent.com/pod-product-compliance
Lightning Source LLC
Chambersburg PA
CBHW011943050726
47590CB00011B/3333